Samantha and Dreamland

Samantha and Dreamland

Irina Shammay

VANTAGE PRESS
New York

This is a work of fiction. Any similarity between the names and characters in this book and any real persons, living or dead, is purely coincidental.

FIRST EDITION

Published by Vantage Press, Inc.
419 Park Ave. South, New York, NY 10016

Manufactured in the United States of America
ISBN: 978-0-533-16005-1

Library of Congress Catalog Card No: 2008901735

0 9 8 7 6 5 4 3 2 1

"Amazing Ricky."
In memory of my loving ferret, Ricky.

Samantha and Dreamland

1

As long as Samantha could recall, she always loved and wished to own a pet. Her father, a man with strong cultural beliefs, opposed the idea of having an animal live in their household. He believed that animals belong to nature's wild and are not to be kept indoors. Samantha's childhood was not so exciting. Her days consisted of books and boring toys rather than a playful pet that she so long yearned for. Among her boring toys, stuffed animals and model guns were Samantha's favorite. At that time, computer games were only in the process of approval.

As if Samantha's life was not miserable enough, her mother added piano lessons to her daily routine. Samantha found her life to be more difficult and annoying. Her mother felt that Samantha was developing boyish behavior. Her beliefs were supported by Samantha's collections of toy guns rather than collectable dolls. Samantha's traits were not what a mother would expect of a daughter. To please Dear Mom, Samantha was spending quality time reading books and playing classical music on the piano.

2

Samantha's family was quite ordinary. As in many traditional families, most of the undivided attention went to the oldest child, in Samantha's case, to her oldest brother, Tom. Even though Tom was seventeen years old, and Samantha was only thirteen, Samantha was smarter and more mature. Being the older sibling in the family has a huge advantage. All your wishes are granted, you can boss your little sister around without any fear of being punished. Samantha often felt jealous of him, wishing she was the only child in the family. Their parents would please him in any possible way, especially Mom. Whatever Tom wanted, he got! If Tom wanted a fish tank, the very next day a big aquarium filled with goldfish would magically appear in his room. Eventually, he would become bored with the goldfish and trade them in for an ugly snake. This kind of action would always go without any discussion or punishment, as he was the favorite. The ugly snake was pleasing to him, as he would scare kids on the block, and later tattle to his friends about it. Tom's othermost enjoyable hobby was giving humorous nicknames to everyone, especially Samantha's friends.

Being the youngest in the family may have its own advantages too, especially if you are much smarter. Samantha decided to manipulate her brother's power to benefit herself. She convinced Tom that life would be so much more exciting if they had a pet living with them. Samantha agreed that she would take good care of it.

There was only problem! Tom was a greedy child. He knew

that Samantha had some savings since she was five years old. But Samantha was determined to have a pet. She figured that she would use half of her savings to bribe her brother and the other half to purchase her pet.

3

Samantha and Tom decided to visit the small pet shop in the neighborhood. While at the pet shop, Samantha learned that her brother disliked dogs, cats, rabbits, mice and birds. She could not find anything that she wanted. She became discouraged and disappointed and she began to cry. Even though Tom and Samantha had had millions of fights before, Tom's coldheartedness would eventually melt when seeing his sister's tears. Once again, Samantha won! "Samantha! Let's go to another store!" Tom said as he was putting his hand on Samantha's left shoulder.

"Where to? The next pet shop is too far!" Samantha sadly responded. "Plus, we need a car; it's a long ride," Samantha added.

"Good thinking, sister! We need a car!" Tom replied.

Samantha started crying even louder, thinking of who could drive them.

"Don't worry, little sister! With my connections we can get anywhere on the map," Tom added. He was so proud of himself. At that moment, Samantha could see his nose all the way up in the air.

What a stuck up, she thought. *Is he for real? How can you get to Africa by car?*

Lucky for Samantha, it turned out to be somewhat true. Tom's friend, James, who was the oldest kid on the block, had a car. He was kind enough to drive them to the main pet store in the next neighborhood.

"This is the hugest pet store I have ever seen in my whole life!" Samantha yelled. Actually, this was the second pet store

Samantha had been to, and indeed, it was the biggest store she had actually seen.

"Close your mouth, sister! Or you will catch a fly," Tom made a funny remark.

The store had all kinds of animals: dogs, cats, hamsters, birds, fish, snakes, hedgehogs, chinchillas, lizards, turtles and many other exotic animals. Walking down the aisle in the store, Samantha noticed a glass box with a few ferrets inside. They were lively playing with each other, except for one. This one was staying far from the others and somewhat staring at Samantha, almost hypnotizing her.

"No! No! No! I am imagining things again!" she said. *How can a ferret stare at me and possibly hypnotize me? Maybe he is sick or even better, he had a bad day. This can happen to the ferret too!* Samantha thought.

Looking at the prices, she noticed that the money she had left was enough to buy a baby hamster with a small cage, but Samantha was not attracted to the hamster. She became even more disappointed and asked her brother if they could go home.

"Do not worry, my little sister! Take back your money and try to find the pet of your dreams," Tom said.

Even though Tom had some plans for tonight with "honestly earned" money, he was somewhat generous. For that moment, Samantha was somewhat proud that he was her older brother.

"I guess you like that rat! So take him. He is somehow staring at you. It is love at first sight!" Tom added with sarcasm.

Tom and his friend started to walk away from Samantha, trying to pick up girls in the store, occasionally teasing birds in the cages. After an approval from the big brother, Samantha started choosing a ferret.

"I need a pet that is happy, playful, smart and definitely healthy. Here are so many ferrets, but this one definitely is staring at me. If I should pick you, nod your head or blink with your left eye right now," Samantha said aloud. "I guess I am getting somewhat crazy since I am talking to him."

Samantha looked at the ferret. Surprisingly for her, he nodded and winked his left eye.

This is weird! Ferrets do not understand humans. Let me try again, she thought.

The same thing happened again. Samantha was shocked. She ran away from the cage and started walking around searching for Tom and his friend. Samantha could not find Tom in the store and decided to go back to the cage. She decided to look at the ferret one more time. Surprisingly for her, he was standing in the same place and staring as before.

"What an ugly ferret you have chosen. Yikes! Looks like a big scary rat!" Tom said with disgust.

"This is my boy! His name is Ricky," Samantha proudly replied to her brother's rude comment.

"You are a special one, I know. A lot of amazing stories are awaiting us!" she said with joy and relief.

"How old are you? Three? Still believing in fairytales. The special one!" Tom added as he circled his finger around his ear implying that Samantha was crazy.

"I do!" Samantha responded, almost crying.

"Tom! Let a kid be a kid. She is only thirteen!" James said in Samantha's defense.

"Thank you for understanding," she replied with appreciation.

"I wish I had a sibling. Being an only child sucks big time," James said with regret and a little jealousy.

"Not!" Tom and Samantha shouted together.

"Think about this, James. Both parents adore you. You can have everything and don't have to share with anyone. It is awesome to be the only child," Tom responded.

"Yeah! He's right," Samantha added with regret that she was Tom's little sister and not an only child in the family. . . .

4

"Do not let him loose in the house! Especially in the living room," Mom yelled, seeing Samantha in the living room playing with Ricky.

"Don't worry, Mom, I am watching him!" Samantha responded.

"You are so cute! Come here," Samantha said with love. Indeed, Ricky was a cute pet with a pinkish nose and black eyes that looked like two small buttons.

The phone rang once, twice . . .

"Mom! The phone is ringing, please pick it up," Samantha begged Mom.

"Samantha, it is for you," Mom yelled back from the kitchen.

"Little fellow! Play in this room and do not make a mess. We do not want to make Mom angry. Believe me you do not want to see that part of Mom. I hope you understand me," Samantha said with hope. The ferret nodded again as if he really understood Samantha.

"I must be imagining things again or maybe I am dreaming? I definitely need a rest. What is going on? I forgot I have someone waiting for me on the phone. I am wondering who it is? Probably Natalie! I wonder what she wants now?" Samantha mumbled as she started walking toward the kitchen to answer the phone. . . .

5

"Good morning, Samantha," the little ferret whispered into Samantha's ear.

"Good morning," Samantha responded. "I must be dreaming, I must be! Ferrets do not speak human," Samantha said and fell asleep.

After a few hours of beauty sleep, Samantha finally woke up and even made her bed without Mom's reminder.

"Where is Ricky? Here you are," Samantha said and patted him on his back.

"It is time to eat!" Samantha rushed down to the kitchen to ask Mom if she could make breakfast.

"Mom! I am so hungry I could eat a horse!" she yelled.

Surprisingly for her there was no response.

Strange! Where is she? Whenever you want to be alone in the house, it is impossible. Now that I need her, she is nowhere to be found, Samantha thought.

"Mom, where are you?" Samantha yelled again, hoping to hear a response. She started to worry. Samantha ran into the living room, the dining room, bathrooms, basement and the yard. Mom was nowhere. Samantha stopped searching and decided to eat a bagel with orange juice.

This is not so bad! Today is Saturday, meaning no school. I can do whatever I want and I am home alone. Yes! Samantha thought.

"Let's go inside Tom's room!" Samantha said to the ferret as she was taking him out of his cage. "I always wanted to see his 'famous' stamp collection. Also, we can search for something intriguing."

After searching Tom's room, goofing around the house and watching TV, Samantha became bored and decided to rest. Walking into her room, Samantha saw little Ricky on the table.

"This is very strange! Why are you on the table?" Samantha said. "This is very strange. Maybe I forgot to put him back into the cage." Samantha started to figure out all the possible explanations of how Ricky could have gotten on the table.

"Go back to your cage!" Samantha commanded.

"Samantha! Stop being bossy!" Ricky responded while standing on his back feet.

"Who is talking to me? I do not recognize this voice," Samantha replied with fear.

"It's me! Ricky! Your ferret!" Ricky responded again.

"Who?" Samantha asked. She was stunned: Ricky can speak!

"This is a miracle! I have a speaking ferret! I am going to be famous! I will be on TV!" Samantha said with hope.

"Samantha! Stop dreaming and come over here," Ricky commanded.

This is scary stuff! Samantha thought as she walked toward Ricky.

"Samantha! Bring me your gold pencil," Ricky commanded before Samantha had a chance to sit down. "It is a magic pencil. Hide it! Never lose it," Ricky added.

"This does not look like a magic pencil. Besides, I do not believe in magic!" Samantha responded.

"So, you do not believe in magic. How would you explain the fact that you are talking to a ferret right now?" Ricky replied.

Samantha posed.

"I do, but I need some reassurance," Samantha said.

"Okay, Samantha! What do you want? Make a wish," Ricky replied, almost smiling.

"Any wish? Any?" she asked.

"Yes!" the ferret responded, almost losing his patience.

"A bicycle, but a beautiful bicycle, like no other," Samantha requested.

"A bicycle it is!" Ricky grabbed the pencil as if it was a magic wand. He commanded Samantha to repeat after him as he waved the wand in circular motions:

"What I wish today, I'll get with this magic wand in hand."

"Circle, circle we go, here's the bicycle that no one owns."

At that instant, many small and shiny sparkles appeared, dancing together in circles. As the stardust diminished, Samantha saw the most beautiful bicycle.

"This is mine?" Samantha asked.

"Yes, it is!" replied Ricky.

"Little Princess Samantha!" Samantha read the label on the bicycle.

Without hesitation, Samantha jumped on the bicycle and began riding with great joy and happiness. She was so preoccupied with her new bicycle that she forgot about the special ferret. Meanwhile, little Ricky was patiently waiting for Samantha to quiet down. . . .

6

Samantha often felt that her parents were not fair to her compared to Tom, especially in reference to bedtime.

Why do I have to go to bed at nine and Tom can stay up? Samantha asked herself. *I guess he is older, he is a boy and more loved by our parents.*

Knowing the unfair outcome of any argument Samantha would have with her parents, she decided to kiss her mom goodnight and went to her room.

"At least somebody loves me and is waiting for me!" Samantha said, thinking about Ricky.

Going up the stairs, Samantha heard her mom's reminder to brush her teeth.

"Samantha, I am coming up in ten minutes to check on you," she added, shouting from the kitchen.

"Love you too, Mom," Samantha replied unhappily.

"Where is my Ricky? Here you are! Do you want to talk?" Samantha asked the ferret. No response. Samantha went to bed, pulled the blanket up to cover her face as if she was hiding from someone.

"Good night, Ricky, and thank you for the bicycle," Samantha whispered. . . .

7

"What a sunny day today! Puffy clouds in the sky!" Samantha said as she stood in front of the window enjoying the view.

"Let's go downstairs and get something to eat," she added.

As Samantha turned, she found herself standing in a ballroom packed with guests. People were dressed in old-fashioned evening attire: some guests were dancing, while others were chatting. Samantha thought she was dreaming. She decided to walk away from the window into the ballroom. As Samantha walked, she noticed that people were staring at her as if she had ten heads. Feeling embarrassed, she ran up the stairs.

"Where is a mirror? I have to see if something is wrong with me?" Samantha asked herself while searching for a mirror. Finally, she found a fancy mirror on a wall.

"Nothing is wrong with me!" Samantha said, looking at the mirror. "I guess my dress is not appropriate for this occasion and my hair is all a mess!" Samantha said unhappily.

"Who are you, young lady?" someone asked Samantha. She saw a funny-looking dwarf standing behind her and impatiently waiting for a response while tapping his left foot.

"My name is Samantha! I do not know how I got here and why? I have a magic pencil that my ferret, Ricky, gave me," Samantha responded, almost defending herself.

"So, you are the one!" the dwarf replied. "I wonder where Ricky is now?"

"Where? He is probably asleep or playing in his box!" Samantha responded.

"In his box?" the dwarf replied, terrified. "Poor fellow," he added with disappointment.

"I do not think so. Anyway, where am I?" Samantha asked the dwarf, trying to change the subject.

"You are at the royal party in honor of Prince David," the dwarf replied with honor. "I suppose he can see you today."

"Great!" Samantha replied.

"Good evening, my friend! I am here!" someone said. Samantha saw the handsome young man who was coming up the stairs toward her.

"Who are you?" Samantha asked.

"Prince David!" the young man replied.

"Your highness! Glad to see you at the ballroom party!" the dwarf said and respectfully bowed.

"Prince?" Samantha asked with surprise.

"Yes! My name is David. I am the Prince of Fairwell Land," the prince responded. "We have to change your looks first before somebody finds out that you are not from here. Then, we can chat more."

"I know I have to change," Samantha replied with sarcasm. "Is it too late for shopping? Plus, I have no money."

Samantha was feeling a bit uncomfortable.

"Where is your gold pencil?" David asked Samantha. "This is not an ordinary pencil. It is the magic wand," the prince added as Samantha took a pencil out of her pocket.

"Now! Samantha, repeat after me," the prince commanded: "Dress me nice to fit the crowd, magic pencil once again."

In an instant, many small particles started to fly around Samantha. As the stardust diminished, her ordinary dress was replaced with a beautiful dress.

"I feel like Cinderella!" Samantha shouted, while attracting attention. She started to breathe harder. Suddenly she felt David's hand holding her hand.

"Now! Let the royal festival begin," David said. . . .

8

Monday. School closed today. Samantha decided to visit Nelly, her best friend since the first grade. Samantha told Nelly all about an amazing purchase she and her brother made. She was thrilled to introduce Ricky to her. Nelly became excited, seeing a speaking ferret and even became speechless for a moment.

"We are rich," both yelled at the same time.

"I forgot to tell you something, Nelly," Samantha added. "I had a strange dream. It was real and magical."

Samantha told Nelly her dream. Obviously, she did not believe a word Samantha was saying and started to laugh. Nelly felt a little bit jealous that Samantha was happy, even in a dream. . . .

9

"Samantha! It is 9 P.M. Time for you to go to sleep," Samantha's mom yelled from downstairs. She also reminded her daughter to wash her face and brush her teeth.

"I know!" Samantha replied with anger. "I cannot wait until I am grown-up."

Samantha washed her face and brushed her teeth. She decided to play with the ferret for a few minutes.

"Before I go to bed, do you want to talk to me?" Samantha asked Ricky.

"Yes, Samantha," the ferret responded. "David really needs you. Only you can help him and save Fairwell Land."

"But how?" Samantha asked, with worries.

"You'll figure it out later," the ferret responded with assurance. "Now remember, the only way you can see the prince is in your dreams. You need to find him as soon as possible. Find him, before it is too late."

"But how? How? I do not understand?" Samantha asked Ricky. She started mumbling and asking many questions.

"Close your eyes, Samantha. My little princess," the ferret added.

"Okay," she responded.

Samantha sent many kisses to Ricky, hugged the pillow and closed her eyes . . .

10

Samantha found herself running alone in a huge green field. She was very happy and enjoyed every minute. Samantha felt very light, as if she was a feather and could fly.

"Strange!" Samantha said to herself. "No parents to obey! No brother to hate! Well, too bad Ricky is not here," she added with some regret.

Samantha was running deeper into a field and found herself in a forest. Walking further into the woods, the forest became darker and scary. Samantha started to worry, wishing that she was home. Suddenly, the ground started to crack and a carriage with two-headed dogs appeared out of the ground. Samantha became speechless. She was not able to run, as if someone was holding her feet. The curtains opened and a face came into sight. A beautiful woman, yet scary and mean, glanced at Samantha.

"Let go already!" somebody yelled from inside the carriage. "There is no time," the same voice added.

The carriage rushed away into the deep forest, as if it had wings.

"I guess I am imagining things again," Samantha said to herself. "I believe that when people are scared, their imagination goes really wild."

Samantha was a brave girl. She knew that she had a mission to complete and somebody needed her help. Slowly, but with confidence, she started walking.

"I am tired, thirsty and hungry! I have no one to talk to, no one to play with. What kind of dream is it?" Samantha said, with disappointment.

After a few minutes of walking, Samantha found herself standing in front of a huge castle. The castle looked as if it was made of small crystals.

This is weird! Samantha thought.

She decided to go inside the castle as she was tired and needed a place to rest. At that time, she had no fear.

"Anyway, this is only a dream. I can always wake up!" Samantha said, trying to calm herself down.

She took a deep breath and started to walk down an alley to the castle. Suddenly, two dwarfs appeared from nowhere.

"Who are you? What business brings you here?" both asked at the same time.

Where did they come from? Samantha asked herself. She noticed that the dwarfs looked like the dwarfs from Prince David's palace.

"Where am I? Who lives here?" she asked.

"You are in the province of Lady Mackflorry," one dwarf replied.

"Make sure she likes you," the other dwarf added.

"What if she doesn't?" Samantha asked with a trembling voice.

"You'll see," the little dwarfs replied while giggling and making scary faces. The dwarfs opened the gate of the castle, allowing Samantha to come in.

As Samantha walked down the hallway, she saw many old paintings and antique sculptures. She felt as if the rooms were alive; pictures and sculptures were bowing and talking to her.

I guess I am so hungry that I am imagining things. This is a mirage! Samantha said to herself as she was walking. . . .

11

It was time to go to school. To avoid humiliation and being laughed at, Samantha decided not to share her dreams with anyone. She impatiently waited for each class to finish, often looking at the clock and counting down the minutes. . . .

"Finally! Home! Sweet home!" Samantha exclaimed.

Evening passed by so fast that Samantha did not realize that it was time to go to bed. . . .

"This is odd!" she questioned herself. "Why do I have strange dreams? Am I a bad person? Why me and the prince?"

Samantha looked at the dream catcher she had on her neck.

"This stuff is not working!" she replied to herself. "Why do I even bother believing in magic."

Suddenly, the dream catcher became alive and started talking.

"Samantha! I know what you are going through. Believe me, I will help you," the dream catcher said, trying to calm Samantha down. "At first, you have to find Prince David and save him from two mean sisters. They are the witches. You must be extremely careful and very cautious," the dream catcher whispered, as if someone was eavesdropping. "Always remember that you have it in yourself and you are the only one who can help David. Follow your heart!" the dream catcher said and turned back into itself. No matter how hard Samantha begged it to speak again, no more was said.

"Fine!" Samantha screamed at the dream catcher and continued walking down the corridor. Samantha was hungry.

All I need is water, she thought. *I can survive without food I guess for many days, but I definitely need water.* Samantha was trying to remember all the facts about water she had learned from the textbooks and television back home.

"What a silly girl!" someone said. "She thinks I am a tree. I hate to break it to you, Samantha, but I need real food. Feed me!"

"Who is this?" Samantha replied with fear. "Who is talking to me?"

Samantha realized that her stomach was talking to her. Her stomach became even hungrier and started to make strange sounds. Samantha became uncomfortable and depressed, wishing she was at home at the dinner table eating a warm meal.

"I got your point!" Samantha yelled. "I see no food here. Let me search the place for it. Just calm down! I can't think with this growling."

"Calm down?" her stomach replied readily. "You never cared for me. Always feeding me junk food."

"Don't even start with me!" she replied, walking even faster.

Samantha saw a giant table full of fruits and berries in the middle of the room. She could bet that the table appeared from nowhere.

"Food!" Samantha exclaimed and ran toward the table. She started eating berries as if she was left without food for days.

"Not too fast. Not too fast," her stomach complained.

I am feeling so light. Something definitely is happening to me? Samantha thought. At that moment, she turned into a beautiful butterfly.

"I am a butterfly! And I can fly," Samantha exclaimed. Without hesitation, she started flying with great joy.

"This place is so huge!" she screamed. "A fountain! A garden! A river!" After a few minutes, Samantha became tired.

"I think I am getting pretty tired. Why am I not a bird? I definitely could fly longer!" she asked herself another question.

Samantha decided to get some rest. She landed on the nearest window. Looking through the window, Samantha saw the same exact dwarfs who earlier welcomed her at the gate. They were making a blend in a big boiling pot.

"Now it's my turn!" one dwarf yelled.

"Be creative this time," the other replied.

A dwarf grabbed a book while searching for the exact page. He started reading a spell. In an instant, many small and shiny sparkles appeared, dancing together in circles. As the stardust diminished, a beautiful little tree appeared.

"What a show! Never saw anything like this!" Samantha said with astonishment.

A dwarf took a few drops from the mixture and splashed them on the tree while saying a different spell. The tree started growing at a fast speed and in a minute, the whole room was filled with it.

"Stop it! Stop it! You fool!" the other dwarf yelled.

"I can't stop it. I don't know how!" the dwarf replied with fear.

The tree started growing even faster and became bigger. The branches had no place in the room, broke the windows and pushed Samantha out.

"What an idiot! An immature magician!" she said with disappointment. *I should fly away before something bad happens to me. By the way, who is Lady Mackflorry?* Samantha thought. *Maybe she knows how to find Prince David! The question was where is she? . . .*

12

Samantha was still amazed by the size of the beautiful garden. The garden was filled with many flowers of playful colors. Samantha had learned that not all flowers were as friendly as they looked; she was almost eaten by a big sleepy-eyed flower.

"Good thing that I am so fast," Samantha said to herself, as she flew away from the big sleepy-eyed flower.

"Wait a minute!" Samantha said to herself. She realized that the garden looked like a gigantic museum filled with beautiful paintings. The wind would make the flowers move to the left, then to the right or up and down. A painting would become alive: here is a woman with a small dog that says "Hi" to you, and there is a black horse nodding its head up and down as it welcomes you.

"This is magic!" Samantha said to herself, repeating the word "magic" again and again. . . .

"Where is Lady Mackflorry? How will I find her?" Samantha said with worries. "If I only had a magic wand, if I only . . ." she paused for a minute. "Wait a minute, I have it."

Samantha realized that she was a butterfly and that her idea about using a magic wand sounded awfully ridiculous and inappropriate at the time.

"I am a butterfly!" Samantha said to herself once again.

She started to worry even more. Samantha decided to ask the flowers in the garden for help. Not every flower in the beautiful garden was honest and told the truth, especially the one who made Samantha sneeze a lot. Finally, with help from purple elephant-ear flowers, Samantha found Lady Mackflorry. The woman was planting flowers in a special pattern, one by one with extreme caution.

"Dear Lady Mackflorry! My name is Samantha," Samantha said.

Samantha paused for a second as she realized that Lady Mackflorry looked exactly like her grandmother.

"Can it be?" Samantha said to herself.

"What an annoying butterfly! My headache is getting even worse," Lady Mackflorry said, and continued to argue with a blue flower about the weather for today.

"She can't see me! I am a butterfly." Samantha said with disappointment. "I need that magic potion to turn myself back." Samantha flew back inside the castle straight into a boiling pot. Using a leaf from a flower in a glass vase, Samantha was able to extract and carry only one drop of magic potion.

Now I have to fly back to see Lady Mackflorry. By the way, what is the life span of a butterfly? Samantha thought and became troubled. She flew as fast as she could, trying to remember anything about a butterfly from her science classes.

"One drop! All I have and all I need," Samantha said, and swallowed a drop to become her normal size again.

"Little girl? Where did you come from?" Lady Mackflorry asked.

"Long story!" Samantha responded. "I need your help."

"First, let's walk," Lady Mackflorry said as she was stretching her legs.

"Can we use magic and fly instead?" Samantha responded.

"Never get used to an easy way, Samantha!" Lady Mackflorry said and grabbed Samantha's hand. "Let's walk and enjoy the sunny day. It will rain soon, news flower told me."

13

Samantha started walking while enjoying the conversation with Lady Mackflorry. As they were passing a strange-looking tree, Samantha felt the leaves of the tree touch and tingle her stomach. As they were passing a river, Samantha felt water drops on her face, as if they were smoothing and calming her down.

"Lady Mackflorry! Do you smell fresh baked pastry?" Samantha asked with hunger.

"Yes, I do. My little helpers bake delicious pastries," Lady Mackflorry responded. "Would you like some? Let's go inside the house."

"What house? There is nothing here!" Samantha said. She did not even finish the sentence, when a beautiful crystal house appeared before her.

"Wow! A magical crystal house again, but how?" Samantha said. "I guess, I am asking too many questions. I am dreaming! Yes, I am! I am at Fairyland."

"Let's sit down at a table and get something to eat," Lady Mackflorry suggested.

Samantha found herself in the middle of a beautiful room. The room was full of candles, flowers and old paintings where people were dining at a table.

"What a beautiful collection of paintings you have!" Samantha said, as she was trying to be polite and appreciative.

Samantha turned to Lady Mackflorry. Instead of an old woman, she found a beautiful woman, looking exactly like her mother.

"Mom? Sorry, Lady Mackflorry," Samantha said while she was staring at Lady Mackflorry. "What is happening? One minute you are an old lady, sorry, next minute you look exactly like my mom?" Samantha added. "I see! Magic is everywhere! No more questions asked."

"Good! Are you hungry, Samantha?" Lady Mackflorry asked.

"Not really!" Samantha responded.

"Liar! Liar!" her stomach reminded Samantha of itself.

"Let's eat," Lady Mackflorry suggested.

Samantha looked at a table with no food on it. In an instant the table became full of different pastries, cookies, candies and fruits.

"Wow!" Samantha added.

As Samantha reached for an apple and was about to eat it, the fruit became alive and screamed.

"Are you crazy? You will eat me up alive? Help! Help!" the apple continued screaming.

"What is going on?" Samantha said and looked at Lady Mackflorry.

"Sorry, Samantha," Lady Mackflorry replied. She put a spell on the food and the food became food again.

"Enjoy and sorry again, Samantha," Lady Mackflorry responded. . . .

14

After a wonderful meal, Samantha started explaining the whole situation to Lady Mackflorry. Samantha was impatiently waiting for a response.

"I need to relax!" Lady Mackflorry finally said. "Samantha, I believe you can play the piano!"

"I do, but only a few simple melodies," Samantha responded. "Sorry. Nothing fancy. I am only a beginner. Plus, I see no piano here."

In an instant, a piano appeared in the middle of the room. Samantha and the chair she was sitting on flew right to the piano at rocket speed.

"Play!" Lady Mackflorry suggested.

Samantha started to play a soft melody that she never knew before. She played it as if she was a great pianist.

"Wow!" Samantha exclaimed. "I am a genius."

"Samantha! Now I need my beauty rest, and I believe you do too," Lady Mackflorry responded while yawning. "Let's talk it over in the morning."

"It will be too late!" Samantha replied with horror.

"Tomorrow! Good night!" Lady Mackflorry added. "By the way, your room is on the left of the corridor."

As Samantha walked down the corridor, she saw more paintings.

Somebody really likes paintings in this house! Samantha thought.

The paintings were somewhat strange. A door in one painting

was closed. A few seconds later, it became wide open, as if it invited you to go in. Then again, it became closed, covered with dust and a spider web as if it was closed for years. The other painting was somewhat amazing. A woman in the painting looked exactly like Lady Mackflorry. A few seconds later, an old woman turned into a beautiful young woman. . . .

"Finally!" Samantha said. "Here is my room."

Samantha found herself inside a small room with a tiny bed. It reminded her of home.

"Good night, Samantha," Lady Mackflorry yelled from the other room. "Did you brush your teeth?"

Strange? Suddenly I feel at home! Samantha thought.

Samantha was trying to fall asleep, but questions were popping up in her head, making it more difficult to fall asleep.

"Stupid clock! Too loud. I can't fall asleep," Samantha said with anger. . . .

15

In the morning, Samantha went to school full of energy, somewhat impatiently waiting for the day to come to an end. Nelly, as usual, was nagging Samantha about her new dream, and Samantha would keep going on and on about a beautiful castle made of crystal. She told Nelly that she played the piano better than any teacher at school and she could prove it.

Samantha and Nelly went inside the auditorium to play the piano. Samantha was trying to remember the melody she played at the magic house, but surprisingly for her, she could not even remember it.

"Strange!" Samantha said. "I swear I was playing almost like our teacher. No, even better."

"Samantha! Wake up!" Nelly replied. "How is Ricky? Can I come over to play with him? Please!" Nelly was waiting impatiently for permission.

"Sure! Anything for my best friend!" Samantha said . . .

16

In the morning, Lady Mackflorry became an old woman again. She told Samantha a scary story about two sisters, the witches, who had two heads and only one body. The witches had an ugly daughter, who most of the time stayed inside a castle. She would occasionally wander in a forest by herself, hiding from people. Samantha also learned that the two witches were jealous of the kingdom of Fairwell Land, as the kingdom was large and beautiful. The sisters were mean. They hated laughter and happy occasions, where they never were invited.

Lady Mackflorry did not know exactly how Samantha could help Prince David. She informed Samantha of the forthcoming party tonight in honor of the twenty-one-year old prince. The king was getting too old to rule the kingdom. He was certain that Prince David was mature enough to be a king. Tradition says the prince has to be married in order to take a kingdom into his hands. Tonight is the night! Prince David has to choose his wife. Many princesses from the different kingdoms will come tonight to be chosen by the prince.

Lady Mackflorry did not know what the two witches had in mind, but she was certain that something bad was about to happen if it was not stopped.

"Samantha!" Lady Mackflorry said. "You need to find out what the two sisters are up to."

"How?" Samantha said with fear. "I am so scared to even think about them, but to go there. Oh, no!"

"You have everything you need in you!" Lady Mackflorry said with faith.

"Whatever you say, Lady," Samantha responded while rolling her eyes.

"We have no time. I will see you at the ball," Lady Mackflorry added.

"What ball?" Samantha asked surprisingly.

"See you later!" Lady Mackflorry said and disappeared, leaving only sparkles in the air. . . .

17

What am I supposed to do now? And where would I find these witches? Samantha thought. She started to worry. "Let's walk, I guess," she said.

"You made a right decision, Samantha!" her stomach said, hoping not to hear more complaints from the girl.

Samantha started to walk down the road, passing a beautiful forest. She saw amazing animals and trees she had never seen before.

"Magic land is amazing!" Samantha said. "I never believed in it! But believe in it and it will come true!" Samantha said to herself.

"Yes! It is!" the dream catcher said. It smiled and became the dream catcher again without any further comment.

As Samantha came to the end of the road, a bookstore appeared.

"Come in! Come in! Buy a book to enjoy!" a dwarf yelled with an annoying voice.

"My ears! It hurts," Samantha yelled with anger.

Samantha did not want to go inside the bookstore, but by some strong and unexplainable power, she was forced to go in.

"Since I have no choice, let's see what this bookstore can offer," Samantha said while trying to calm herself down.

Samantha picked up a book from the second shelf. Instantly, the empty space on the shelf was occupied with the same book.

"Wow!" Samantha said. "This could be great for my library."

Samantha opened the book in the middle. Suddenly, an angry

goblin started to walk inside the book while screaming and destroying everything in his way.

"What are you looking at?" he yelled at Samantha.

Samantha slammed the book shut with horror. After a few minutes, she decided to open the book again. This time she saw a forest and heard somebody crying.

I think somebody is hurt and needs help! Samantha thought. She placed her hand on the page and realized that her hand was inside the book.

"Wait a minute. I can go inside?" Samantha said and slowly placed her arm inside the book. In an instant, Samantha found herself in a forest. She started walking. Crying sounds became closer and closer. Samantha approached a girl near a river who was staring at her reflection in the river and crying.

"Who are you? Why are you crying?" Samantha asked the stranger.

"Please go away. I am so ugly," the girl responded.

Samantha looked at the girl. The girl had a big nose and scary-looking teeth. In addition, she had a small hump on her back.

Strange! She looks somewhat like Nelly, Samantha thought. "Wait a minute! Nelly is not ugly, yet there is some resemblance!" Samantha imagined how a girl would look with blond and curly hair, with a different colored dress. Samantha pulled a magic wand out her pocket and waved it at the girl while saying a spell:

What was once dark and black, it becomes bright and blond,
Color, color, dress with color, ugly girl will see no more.

In an instant her dark and sticky hair became blond and shiny; her dark and ugly dress suddenly was replaced by a beautiful one.

The girl looked into the river and saw a cute girl. Nothing actually changed, except her dress and hair.

"Wow! This is me and I am cute!" the girl said with great joy and happiness. She ran to Samantha and started spinning her around.

"Put me down! Put me down!" Samantha demanded. "I am getting dizzy."

The girl, who called herself Strashna, told Samantha that she was the daughter of two sisters, the witches. The girl, a young lady aged seventeen, was deeply in love with the Prince of Russava, Charles. Strashna found out that her mothers had a different future life planned for her, and definitely not with Prince Charles.

Strashna asked Samantha to turn her back before the two witches would see her. . . .

18

"What a strange book!" Samantha said.

The book had all the dwellers of Fairwell Land, including the two witches. Samantha was too horrified to open the book and decided to leave the shop. The dream catcher became alive again and insisted that Samantha open the book.

"I am really scared and I am not going in there!" Samantha said with horror.

"Use your magic! Be a butterfly! Fly into the book!" the dream catcher suggested.

"What a great idea!" Samantha responded. "Why did I not think of it? I guess I am too slow when I am scared."

"Maybe!" the dream catcher added with sarcasm.

"By the time I get the magic potion, it will be too late!" Samantha responded with disappointment.

"Use your magic wand, Samantha," the dream catcher said.

"What? Where have you been before?" Samantha responded.

She pulled the magic wand out of her pocket and said the spell. Instantly, the bottle with the magic potion appeared in Samantha's hand.

Wow! Magic! I better enjoy the magic before it becomes real and boring, Samantha thought. She opened the page, quickly drank the magic potion and became a butterfly.

"Let's do it!" Samantha screamed.

It was dark, almost impossible to fly and to see.

"I wonder if I can use the magic wand?" Samantha asked herself while reaching into her pocket for the wand.

"Magic!" Samantha said.

She waved the magic wand and the pathway became light and bright. Samantha was flying and flying, but the two witches were nowhere to be found. As Samantha was getting tired, she decided to fly on the porch of the two witches' castle to get some rest. Suddenly, the two-headed scary dogs appeared and started barking. Horrified, Samantha flew inside the castle. After a few minutes of calming down, she decided to explore the place. Suddenly, she heard voices coming from behind.

"I am so hungry! Let's eat," one witch said to the other.

"First, let's discuss our plan," the other replied.

"Very well! Why do I have the strong feeling that somebody is here?" she asked with suspicion.

"You are paranoid as usual!" the other sister said. "Who can possibly come to our place? We do not have any friends. Strangers will not come here. We have the two-headed dogs, the hungry tree and many other guards. Just relax and enjoy your food."

"The two-headed dog I saw. Scary! What were they saying about other guards and a tree?" Samantha whispered with horror.

"Do not worry! We are next to you," the stomach and the dream catcher responded in one voice.

"Oh, yes! You are my saviors!" Samantha responded with sarcasm. . . .

19

Samantha was patiently sitting on a picture frame, waiting for the two-headed witches to finish eating.

"I am almost done eating. How about you, sister?" one witch asked.

"I am done too! I would like to eat fruit now. How about you?" the other responded.

"Servants!" one of the witches yelled out loud.

Two dwarfs appeared.

"Strange. All dwarfs in Fairyland look alike," Samantha said and paused for minute.

"We are here to obey and to please you, your majesty. What is the request?" the two dwarfs replied together while shivering and horrified.

"Bring me fruit and right away," one of the witches yelled while the sister giggled too loud, making Samantha fall down from the picture frame.

"Obeying and pleasing, your majesty," the two dwarfs walked away and in an instant came back with fruit.

"Why don't they use their magic to get food. They like to abuse us!" one dwarf whispered to the other with anger.

"Don't ask stupid questions, you fool," the other dwarf replied with fear. "Just obey. Remember what happened to our brother?"

"Please, don't remind me," the other dwarf whispered.

"I think I am done eating," one witch said.

"Me too," the other witch responded.

"Let's do it," the witches said together.

The two-headed sisters started walking down toward the garden. Samantha was patiently following them. Suddenly, a two-headed tree appeared from nowhere and bowed to them. Samantha became horrified; she remembered what the witches previously said about guards. The tree became alive and scary. It started to move while trying to catch a fly by making hands out of leaves.

"Who is here?" one witch said with suspicion and looked back at a tree.

"Nobody! Perhaps a fly!" the other witch responded. "You know how a tree hates flies."

Samantha became weak as she was struggling with the tree. Finally, she pulled herself together and flew away from the scary tree. As the two sisters walked further down into the forest, Samantha realized that she was getting more tired. The two sisters kept walking and walking until they came to an open field. Patiently Samantha continued to follow them as a shadow.

"I have a feeling that I have been here before," Samantha said to herself. "But I can't remember."

A small dark house appeared from nowhere.

What a magical land! Everything appears from nowhere! Samantha thought.

The house was scary-looking, old and had no windows. The door opened and the two-headed witches walked inside. Samantha was about to fly inside, but the door closed and the house disappeared.

"What am I supposed to do now?" Samantha asked herself, while hoping that the dream catcher or stomach would suggest something.

After a few minutes of wondering and hoping. Samantha decided to fly out of the book. . . .

20

"Good morning, Samantha! Time to go to school!" Samantha's mother whispered into her left ear.

"I didn't find out anything. What was I supposed to do?" Samantha said, still dreaming.

"What are you talking about, Samantha? Did you have a bad dream again? We had better see the psychic reader or better yet, make an appointment to see my shrink," Samantha's mother added with worry.

"Good morning, Mom!" Samantha responded and stretched her arms. "Do not worry! Everything is under control! It is morning and I am here, not in the scary kingdom of the two-headed witches."

"What are you talking about?" Samantha's mom said. . . .

21

Today was a fun day at school; today was "My Pet Day." Students were allowed to bring a pet to school for an introduction. Samantha was very excited. She even forgot to eat breakfast before going to school.

"Where are you taking that ugly ferret?" Tom asked with curiosity.

"You are ugly! He is cute!" Samantha replied and kissed the ferret.

Many students have dogs, cats and hamsters. Samantha was proud that she was the one who had a ferret. Each student was given a fifteen-minute presentation about their pet. Samantha talked about her ferret with such passion and love that everyone just kept listening and listening without interruption, even though she went over the given time.

After dinner, Samantha came to her mother and started a strange conversation.

"Mom! I have a question for you," Samantha said. "Are you really happy with Dad? Would you change anything about your marriage? Do you really love Dad?"

"What's got into you?" her mother responded suspiciously. "Where are you getting these strange questions?"

"You see, Mom, a lot of questions have been piling up inside my head. I need some answers," Samantha said.

"It is too early for you to know the answers to these questions," her mom replied.

"You will not tell me the right answers?" Samantha said, almost demanding.

"I will tell you the following: love is very unique. There are no right or wrong answers to your questions. You are the one who knows the right answers, but it is still too early for you to know," Mom said, trying to please Samantha with her response. "As for me and your dad, I am happy! I would change nothing, except for you not to be so nosy."

"Mom! I am serious!" Samantha complained.

"Me too," Mom added. . . .

22

Meanwhile, the two-headed sisters were reading a spell book. They planned to marry off Strashna to Prince David, so later on the two witches would take the Kingdom of Fairwell Land into their hands. The question was how to make Prince David fall in love with Strashna? They knew that their daughter was deeply in love with Prince Charles. His kingdom was too small, and Prince Charles had two older brothers to be kings before him. The two sisters could not tolerate Strashna and Charles being together and decided to break them up. For many years, the witches were jealous of Fairwell Land. This was a great opportunity for their dream to come true.

The sisters had a plan: they prepared a spell potion for Strashna to drink at the ball. The potion would make Strashna forget about Prince Charles for good. The same potion would be given to Prince David. It would make him fall in love with Strashna. Even though she was an ugly-looking girl, he would not see it. He would be under the spell of the potion and will fall in love with her.

"Your ideas are always great, sister!" one witch said, complimenting the other. "What would I do without you?"

"One head is good, but two heads are better!" the other sister replied.

"Now! There is one problem: Prince David and Strashna have to drink the spell potion at the same time," one witch said.

"But how?" the other sister replied.

"I believe I have a solution!" one witch said. "Servants!" she yelled.

Two dwarfs appeared.

"We are here to serve and to obey you, your majesty!" the dwarfs said together.

The witch stared at the servants as if she was studying them.

"Please tell me your idea, sister!" the other witch asked impatiently.

"All dwarfs in Fairwell Land look alike!" one witch said. "But, each dwarf has a different place to live and a different outfit to wear. Our dwarfs will serve tonight at the ball. All we have to do is dress them like the servants of Fairwell Land."

"They will serve Strashna and Prince David the spell potion at the same time!" the other with responded. "You are indeed a genius!"

The two-headed sisters gave detailed instructions to the dwarfs. They also reminded the dwarfs of what might happen if they disobey.

"I am so scared. I barely can walk," one dwarf said to the other.

"I can't take this anymore! I have to do something! I am so fed up with these orders! I want to be free and to serve the king and Prince David of Fairwell Land," the other dwarf responded.

"Shut up, you fool! They can read your mind," the other dwarf whispered.

"They are busy with their plan and they don't care about anything at this moment," the dwarf responded. . . .

23

"Today is the ball!" Samantha said to herself. "How should I dress? I have no dress." Samantha became paranoid and decided to go to the bookstore at Fairwell Land to seek a possible solution.

Samantha was trying to find the way to the store, but unsuccessfully. She pulled the magic wand out of her pocket, whispered the magic words and found herself inside the bookstore.

"Again, the annoying voice!" Samantha said to herself and started walking toward a dwarf. "I need a lovely dress for the ball."

"You are at the bookstore, not the dress store," a dwarf replied and started laughing. "Use your magic wand!"

"I tried, but it isn't working!" Samantha responded.

"I know. You cannot use the magic wand for your personal request. Sorry! But, I might have a solution for you," the dwarf said. "Go to aisle 246810, shelf number 5."

"What?" Samantha asked.

"Just go!" the dwarf replied impatiently.

Samantha looked up to see what aisle she was standing next to.

"This must be a joke! Number 2!" Samantha screamed. "Wait a minute! What aisle number 246810? There are only ten aisles."

"I just hate guests who know absolutely nothing and will not even try to think!" a dwarf replied, almost yelling. "Your aisle is 246810, meaning, you have to walk past aisle 2, then 4, then 6, then 8, then 10."

"Thank you!" Samantha said. *What an unpleasant dwarf! He*

reminds me of Arthur, the next-door kid, Samantha thought. She visualized Arthur at school with his unhappy facial expression and started walking.

As Samantha was passing the book aisles, she heard different voices talking to her.

"Take me, Samantha, I will teach you black magic," one book said.

"Take me, Samantha, I will teach you how to cook," another book said.

"I am hallucinating! I must be tired or hungry," Samantha said to herself. She was tempted by the voices and by what they were offering, but decided not to stop.

"Finally! Aisle number 10," Samantha said with relief.

She found herself standing in front of the long aisle. Samantha found shelf number 5. Surprisingly, all the books on the shelf had no titles.

"Too many books and too little time! How will I find the right book?" Samantha asked herself with disappointment.

"The girl isn't too bright when pressured," the dream catcher whispered to the stomach with disappointment.

"I think it is time to use the magic wand," Samantha said out loud for the dream catcher and the stomach to hear, pretending she did not hear the hurtful comment.

Samantha reached for the magic wand and said the spell. Instantly, a book rushed down from the shelf as if it was alive and had arms and legs.

Immediately, Samantha found herself at a runway show for evening gowns.

"Ladies and gentlemen! I am glad to begin the show in the honor of our special guest, Samantha," the dwarf announced. The audience applauded. The show started. As the models came close to the first row, Samantha noticed that all the models looked exactly like her.

"This is amazing! Only in the magic land is everything possible!" Samantha said with excitement. "All the dresses are beautiful! I need one, which one, which one?" Samantha said and started to panic as any girl would do in this situation.

Samantha's helplessness in deciding which dress to choose drove the dream catcher and stomach mad. They tried to help Samantha in choosing a dress, but Samantha was not fully satisfied with what she saw. She wanted something extraordinary.

"I think I know who can help me! The fashion advisor!" Samantha said to herself. She reached for the magic wand and said the spell. Instantly, two dwarfs appeared.

"Here to serve you as fashion advisors," the dwarfs said together.

"Strange! I expected Marilyne Sortore or Demolishe Kabotinetre! They are well known as fashion advisors," Samantha said with disappointment.

The two dwarfs whispered something and a beautiful dress appeared.

"Wow!" Samantha screamed with happiness and joy. The dress was beautiful, stunning and dazzling. Samantha put on the dress.

I wonder, can I wear this dress to my graduation dance? Samantha thought. *Can I have a picture of it? I guess not.*

Samantha looked at the mirror and could not believe how beautiful and gorgeous she looked. Samantha started waltzing by herself. She came to the mirror to see herself one more time and became speechless:

"Who are you?" Samantha asked. She saw a beautiful young lady, age sixteen in the mirror. "I guess, this is me! This is how I will look in the future, beautiful and charming," Samantha said while enjoying what she saw. "What is happening to me? Did I spend four years here?" Samantha added while hyperventilating.

"Relax, Samantha! You are in Fairyland and everything is possible here," the stomach said, trying to calm Samantha down. . . .

24

"Samantha! It is time to go to school!" Mom yelled from downstairs.

"I am already up," Samantha responded with a sleepy voice.

"School! School! I want to be a grown-up already," Samantha said to herself and started wondering. "I remember that I was a beautiful sixteen-year-old young lady in my dream. I was indeed a beauty. Now I am myself again and have to go to school."

Samantha did not want to go to school. She had no choice. She brushed her teeth, then ate breakfast very slowly, hoping for a miracle to happen so that she could skip school. Nothing happened. Nothing major happened at school, still the same boring routine for Samantha. Time to go to bed.

"Good night, Mom," Samantha said. "Good night, Ricky," she added and closed her eyes. . . .

25

Once again, Samantha found herself standing at the stairs of the ballroom. Now, she was a sixteen-year-old beautiful young lady. Samantha recognized the soft and kind voice of Prince David behind her. She blushed, felt her blood rushing through the veins and arteries in her body.

"Who are you, oh beautiful young lady?" Prince David asked.

"My name is Samantha," she responded, almost whispering.

Prince David asked Samantha to dance. She was overwhelmed.

"What a beautiful night! A night to remember forever!" Samantha said with excitement and happiness. . . .

26

At the same time, two horrified servants of the two-headed witches were following instructions with extreme caution. Each was holding a glass with the magic potion. They were shivering from fear, occasionally spilling the potion on the floor.

"Now or never!" one dwarf whispered to the other.

"What again! Are you crazy? Do you want to die?" the other dwarf responded.

"I would rather die than be an unhappy servant for the rest of my life!" the dwarf said with honor.

"Do you have a plan?" the other dwarf asked.

Indeed, the dwarf had a brilliant yet dangerous plan. He decided to inform Prince Charles about the vicious plan of the two-headed witches. The dwarfs would switch the magic potion with fruit juice. Later, they would serve it to Prince David and Strashna.

"Now or never?" the dwarf asked again.

"Now!" the other dwarf replied.

As agreed, one dwarf rushed to Prince Charles. Even though the prince was strictly forbidden to see Strashna, without any hesitation he went to the ball to save his love. He could not believe that the mothers would use their daughter to benefit themselves. Yet, he knew they were evil.

Meanwhile, the two-headed witches decided to disguise themselves by being a beautiful one-headed woman, hiding their second head behind hair.

"I can barely breathe!" one sister complained. "Hair makes it almost impossible to breathe."

"Be strong, my sister!" the other said with understanding.

The two witches started to walk down the corridor, smiling to other guests, trying to be friendly. One sister was holding a two-headed cat in her right hand. It was a custom for well-known ladies to carry a cat in their hand at the ball.

"I believe everything is ready?" one witch asked her servant with anger.

"Of course, your majesty!" a dwarf replied.

"Where is our daughter?" the other witch asked and started to look for their daughter.

"Find her!" the other witch ordered the dwarf.

At the same time, Samantha was looking for Strashna.

"Here you are!" Samantha said with great relief. She pulled Strashna to the corner away from other guests.

"Now it is time for magic!" Samantha said and pulled out the magic wand. Once again, she turned Strashna into a beautiful young lady.

"You are so beautiful, Strashna!" Samantha said, trying to compliment her. "Let's go to the ballroom."

Samantha and Strashna went straight to the ballroom.

"I would love Prince Charles to see me right now!" Strashna said. "If he could see me like this, I know he will love me forever!"

Prince Charles was standing right behind her and heard her words.

"I am here, my love!" Prince Charles said.

Strashna was overwhelmed and happy. She ran into his arms and kissed him. Prince Charles told Strashna about the plan the two witches had. She was somewhat disappointed and could not believe it. Yet, she knew they were mean witches.

27

Prince David was looking for Samantha, the beautiful young lady who stole his heart for the rest of his life.

"May I have this dance?" Prince David asked Samantha.

"With pleasure!" she responded.

While dancing, Samantha told Prince David everything she knew about the vicious plan of the two-headed witches. He was furious and had a plan of his own for a payback.

"Let's act calm, not to attract anybody's attention!" Samantha suggested.

28

The dwarfs switched the spell potion with the harmless fruit juice beforehand and were waiting for the command.

"It is time!" the two-headed witches commanded their dwarfs.

As agreed, the dwarfs gave one glass of potion to Prince David and one to Strashna to drink at the same time. The two-headed witches were impatiently waiting for the potion to work; for Prince David and Strashna to fall madly in love with each other. Nothing happened.

"What is going on?" one witch yelled aloud, almost scaring the guests away.

Prince David asked beautiful Samantha to dance and Strashna started dancing with Prince Charles.

"What is happening? What is happening?" the witch yelled again.

One of the dwarfs started to laugh. He was very happy, like never before.

"You are a traitor! You will be punished! All of you!" the witch said with anger.

Guests started to laugh along with the dwarf, without understanding his joy. The two-headed witches became angry. The second head came out of the hair. Everyone became horrified by the unwelcome guests and stopped laughing. They recognized the two-headed witches.

"You will be punished!" one witch said to the dwarf. She threw magic dust on one of the dwarfs and turned him into a ferret.

The ferret made a circle and disappeared. The guests were scared and started to panic.

"You! You will be an ugly pig!" the other witch shouted at Prince David. She was about to turn him into a pig, but he was lucky that Lady Mackflorry appeared from nowhere.

"You aren't welcomed here! Leave us at once!" Lady Mackflorry said with a strong and assertive voice.

"Try to stop us! We are much stronger than we were before! You can't defeat us!" one witch responded. The two-headed witches threw lightning at Lady Mackflorry, but it reflected back at them. Then Lady Mackflorry started to put a spell on the two witches. Instantly, the two-headed witches started to shrink to the size of a mouse.

"You can't do this to us!" the two-headed witches replied with squeaky voices.

"Sorry! I just did!" Lady Mackflorry said with relief.

"We are too small!" one witch said with disappointment.

"I know. Just pray that our cat isn't around," the other witch replied.

"Where is the two-headed cat? Come here! Come here!" Lady Mackflorry called the cat.

"I feel that somebody is breathing right behind me," one sister whispered to the other.

"Run!" the witches screamed as they were running away from the two-headed cat.

What exactly happened to the two-headed witches, nobody knows for sure. . . .

29

Samantha was standing in front of a beautiful fountain. She was a sixteen-year-old young and happy lady, who was in love with handsome Prince David. Lady Mackflorry appeared from no-where.

"I have a question for you, Samantha," she said. "Would you want to stay here forever with Prince David or would you rather go back home to your family?"

Samantha stopped breathing for a minute. Teardrops rushed down from her beautiful green eyes.

"Home? I totally forgot about it! Mom and Dad! Tom and friends!" Samantha whispered.

Samantha totally forgot about her past. She started believing in her own lies, that she was a sixteen-year-old young girl living in Fairwell Land all her life.

"I am not sixteen! I am only thirteen!" Samantha said with disappointment. "This isn't my real life. Mom and Dad! I really miss you!"

"You have to go home," Lady Mackflorry said. "Somebody needs your help there.

"You have to help a dwarf to become a dwarf again, so he can enjoy being free in Fairwell Land," Lady Mackflorry added. "Samantha, I am referring to your ferret, Ricky! He is impatiently waiting for you."

"Go home and forget about Fairyland?" Samantha asked.

"We are always together! We are not saying 'Farewell,' we

are just saying 'Good-bye,' Samantha!" Lady Mackflorry said while gently patting Samantha on her back.

"But how will I turn Ricky back into a dwarf?" Samantha asked, trying to be brave and strong while wiping teardrops from her face.

Lady Mackflorry whispered the spell into Samantha's left ear for no one to hear. Samantha said "Good-bye" to all of the dwellers of Fairyland, kissed Prince David and promised to come back soon. . . .

30

In the morning, Samantha rushed to see her ferret while repeating the spell so as not to forget it.

"Strange! The spell is not working. I probably forgot some words?" Samantha said and panicked. "Let me try again."

She said the spell repeatedly. Nothing happened. Samantha started talking to the ferret. Surprisingly, the ferret did not respond.

"Are you mad at me, my little fellow? Talk to me, please!" Samantha said repeatedly, louder and louder.

Tom became annoyed by the loud voice of his sister.

"What is going on, Samantha? Are you out of your mind? Talking to a ferret?" Tom yelled, barely restraining himself.

"Nothing!" Samantha replied.

"My friend and I are working on our class project. Can you calm down already?" Tom demanded.

"Who is with you?" Samantha asked and walked into Tom's room. She was amazed by what she saw: Tom's friend looked exactly like Prince David.

"Is your name David?" Samantha asked.

"No. My name is Jim! I am new to the neighborhood," the young boy responded. "How are you doing?"

"Fine, I think!" Samantha replied.

"Samantha! What are you doing here? Mom!" Tom yelled for Mom's help.

"Don't you worry! I am leaving!" Samantha replied, barely holding back her tears. She walked back to her room.

"Is it possible that I was dreaming?" Samantha asked herself.

All day Samantha was sitting and thinking over and over of what might've gone wrong.

Why didn't the spell work? Did I forget some words? Maybe I was dreaming and imagined everything? she thought.

"Time to go to bed," Mom yelled from downstairs.

"I am already in bed," Samantha replied.

"Good night, my little friend, and sweet dreams!" Samantha said to the ferret. She was almost certain that Ricky blinked his left eye.

"I can hardly wait to fall asleep and to be around my friends," she said and fell asleep. . . .